MARGRET & H. A. REY'S
Curious George
at the Baseball Game

Written by Laura Driscoll

Illustrated in the style of H. A. Rey by Anna Grossnickle Hines

Houghton Mifflin Company   Boston

www.hmhbooks.com

The text of this book is set in Adobe Garamond
The illustrations are watercolor.

Library of Congress Cataloging-in-Publication Data

Driscoll, Laura.
Margret & H. A. Rey's Curious George at the baseball game / by Laura Driscoll ; illustrated in the style of H. A. Rey by Anna Grossnickle Hines.
p. cm.
Summary: Curious George and the man with the yellow hat attend a baseball game to cheer on the Mudville Miners.
ISBN 0-618-66375-4 (pbk. : alk. paper) — ISBN 0-618-66374-6 (hardcover)
[1. Baseball—Fiction. 2. Monkeys—Fiction.] I. Title: Curious George at the baseball game. II. Rey, Margret. III. Rey, H. A. (Hans Augusto), 1898–1977. IV. Hines, Anna Grossnickle, ill. V. Title.
PZ7.D79Mar 2006
[E]—dc22
2005013426

Hardcover ISBN-13: 978-0618-66374-3
Paperback ISBN-13: 978-0618-66375-0

Manufactured in China
SCP 18 17 16 15 14 13
4500430942

This is George.

He was a good little monkey and always very curious.

Today George and the man with the yellow hat were going to the ballpark to watch a baseball game. George couldn't wait to see what it would be like.

At the baseball stadium, the man with the yellow hat introduced George to his friend, the head coach of the Mudville Miners. He had arranged for George to watch the game from the dugout. What a treat! George got a Miners cap to wear. Then he sat on the bench with the players. He felt just like part of the team!

The players cheered a Miners home run. George cheered, too.

The players groaned at a Miners strikeout. George groaned, too.

Then George noticed one of the Miners coaches making funny motions with his hands. He touched his cap. He pinched his nose. He dusted off his shoulder.

Hmm, thought George. Maybe this was another way to cheer on the team.

So George made some hand motions, too. He tugged at his ear.

He rubbed his tummy.

He scratched his chin.

Just then, a Miners player got tagged out at second base. The player pointed at George. "That monkey!" he said. "He distracted me with his funny signs."

Oops! The coach had been giving directions to the base runner. George's hand signals had taken his mind off the play. Poor George! He had only been trying to be part of the team. Instead the Miners had lost a chance to score.

George watched the rest of the game from a stadium seat. Or at least he *tried* to watch the game. There was so much going on around him.

There was food for sale.

There were shouting fans.

There was a woman holding a big camera . . .

The woman pointed her camera at some fans. And look! Those fans waved out from the huge screen on the ballpark scoreboard.

George had never been on TV before. He was very curious.
What would it be like to see himself on the big screen?

13

He soon learned the answer: it was exciting!

2 BALL 0 STRIKE 1 OUT

MINERS	0	0	1	2				
ROCKETS	0	1	0					

George liked seeing himself on the screen.

"Hey, you!" shouted the camerawoman. "Cut that out!"

Uh-oh! George had gotten a little carried away. He ran off, with the angry camerawoman hot on his heels.

In the busy stadium breezeway, George hid behind a popcorn cart. He waited for the camerawoman to pass by.

Just then, George heard a noise behind him. It was a quiet little noise—like a sigh, or a sniff. What could have made that noise? George wondered.

George turned. There, behind the cart, was a little boy, crying. George wanted to help. He crept out of his hiding place and over to the boy.

"Ah-ha! There you are!" shouted the camerawoman, spotting George. Then the camerawoman noticed the teary-eyed boy. She seemed to forget that she was mad at George.

"I'm lost," the boy said. "I can't find my dad."

If only there were a way to let the boy's dad know where he was. But there *was* a way! The camerawoman aimed her lens at the little boy, and . . .

there he was on the big screen for everyone to see—including his dad.

Within minutes, the boy and his father were together again and the man with the yellow hat had come to find George.

"I can't thank you enough," the boy's father said to the camerawoman.

The camerawoman shrugged. "Don't thank me," she said. She patted George on the back. "It was this little fellow who found your son."

George was the star of the day.